Y0-DWP-897

You Can Make Magic!
in
Blackstone's Magical Adventures

Harry Blackstone, Jr., is one of the greatest magicians in the world today. In the magical adventure that you and he will share, you help him to solve mysteries, to help out people in trouble, and you get to learn and do real magic tricks, too!

A special world of fun and thrills begins in each new book. You decide which way to go, which clues to follow. You are the real hero in the story!

If you follow a path that leads to trouble, you can always change your mind and try another way, turn a different page. And each new adventure will teach you magic tricks that you can show your friends. You can be a magician, just like Blackstone!

Plus, there's a special Blackstone Picture Trick in the back of each book, with step-by-step instructions for making magic.

But you can't start your adventure until you start reading. Better turn to page 5. You don't want to waste a minute of fun!

Look for these Magical Adventure books from Tor

BLACKSTONE'S MAGICAL ADVENTURE #1:
  AMERICA'S SECRET KING
BLACKSTONE'S MAGICAL ADVENTURE #2:
  THE SECRETS OF STONEHENGE

BLACKSTONE'S MAGICAL ADVENTURE
THE SECRETS OF STONEHENGE

NUMBER TWO   MILO DENNISON

Illustrated by Paul Abrams

TOR

A TOM DOHERTY ASSOCIATES BOOK

Blackstone is a trademark of Blackstone Magik Enterprises, Inc.
© 1986 Blackstone Magik Enterprises, Inc. Under exclusive license
from Larido Merchandising, Inc. All rights reserved.

This is a work of fiction. All the events and characters, with the
exception of Harry Blackstone, Jr., portrayed in this book are fictional,
and any resemblance to real people or incidents is purely coincidental.

BLACKSTONE'S MAGICAL ADVENTURE #2:
THE SECRETS OF STONEHENGE

Copyright © 1986 by Tom Doherty Associates, Inc.

All rights reserved, including the right to reproduce this book or
portions thereof in any form.

First printing: November 1986

A TOR Book

Published by Tom Doherty Associates, Inc.
49 West 24 Street
New York, N.Y. 10010

ISBN: 0-812-56259-3
CAN. ED.: 0-812-56260-7

Printed in the United States of America

0 9 8 7 6 5 4 3 2 1

It was the first day of summer vacation and the Kingsley family was seated around the dinner table. Mr. Kingsley was as happy as Tom and Alice, his son and daughter. He was a high school history teacher so he had the summer off too.

"I've decided that I'm really going to do it," Mr. Kingsley said.

"Going to do what, Dad?" asked Alice.

"I'm going to England to see Stonehenge," Mr. Kingsley replied.

"Stonehenge, what's that?" Tom asked.

"It's an ancient stone ruin that the Druids used for their ceremonies," said Mr. Kingsley.

"What are Druids?" Alice asked.

"The Druids," said Mr. Kingsley, "were people who lived all over Europe thousands of years ago. They believed that sacred spirits lived in trees and stones—particularly large stones. The Druids disappeared, or at least they seemed to, a long time ago. But I think they are still around, probably near Stonehenge. That's why I'm going there, or I should say that's why the three of us are going there."

"The three—" Alice started.

"I'm going back to school for the summer," Mrs. Kingsley interrupted. "It will help me get a better position at the library. You and Tom will go with your father."

"It will be a fun vacation," said Mr. Kingsley. "You'll learn a lot about England and we may also run into Mr. Blackstone."

"Your friend, Blackstone the magician?" Tom exclaimed.

"The one and only," said Mr. Kingsley. "He is

giving a performance for the royal family, and he has promised to join us at Stonehenge. The Druids are believed to have had magical powers and Blackstone is interested in them also."

A few days later, Mr. Kingsley, Tom, and Alice boarded a plane to England.

After the plane landed, they all took a taxicab to Waterloo Station in London where they boarded a train. After an hour and a half they arrived in Salisbury, the large city nearest to Stonehenge. From there, they went by rented car to Amesbury, a town only a couple of miles from Stonehenge itself.

"This is where we are going to stay," said Mr. Kingsley as the small English car they were driving came to a stop in front of a two-story building in the center of town.

"Do you think any Druids live in there?" Alice asked in a whisper.

"If they do," said Mr. Kingsley, laughing, "they will be disguised as bellboys."

There weren't any bellboys, but Mr. Bloomfield, the owner of the hotel, checked them in and showed them to their rooms.

"The car we rented wasn't running very smoothly on the way here," said Mr. Kingsley. "I'd better find a garage and have it checked over. I saw a garage just outside of town. You two stay close by until I come back. I don't think I'll be very long. Then we can go for a long drive in the countryside."

The car with Mr. Kingsley went sputtering off down the street.

Tom and Alice took a walk through the narrow but sunny streets of the small town. When they got back

to the hotel, they expected to find their father waiting there for them.

"I don't think he's come back yet," said Mr. Bloomfield. "Often these car repairs take much longer than you think they will."

"Do you think we should go and look for him?" asked Alice. "The garage can't be that far out of town."

If they go looking for Mr. Kingsley, turn to page 11.

If they stay at the hotel and wait for him to come back, turn to page 28.

Blackstone landed his plane at the Salisbury airport. Then, he went into the administration building followed by Tom and Alice.

"We'll send a rescue helicopter over to see if old McInter is all right," said the airport official.

"McInter?" Blackstone asked.

"Ian McInter," said the official, "used to stage mock aerial dogfights with another World War II fighter plane for the tourists. Used blank bullets, of course. The other pilot gave it up and retired. McInter refuses to. Sorry if he gave you a scare. We're quite used to him around here. Anything I can help you with?"

"I'm trying to find my father," Alice said. "He came over here to study Stonehenge and now we can't find him."

"Ah, Stonehenge," said the official. "It's a hobby of mine also. I even dress up like a Druid now and then—for the pageants, you know. If your father is missing, we'll find him soon enough. Let's start by taking you over to Stonehenge right now."

THE END

Tom and Alice started walking in the direction of the garage. They soon left the small town behind and found themselves in a countryside of well-kept fields and cows. The road stretched ahead into a broad plain.

They walked for what seemed like hours. They were about to give up and start back, when they saw a row of cars along the road and a large building next to them. There was a man sitting by the open garage door.

"We're looking for our father," Tom said a little out of breath. "He's driving a small red car."

"Somebody brought in a car like that a few hours ago," said the man. "It wasn't running too well, but I found the trouble and he continued on toward Salisbury."

"Did he say anything?" Alice asked. "I mean about why he was going there."

"No, he didn't say anything," said the garage man, "but he did sign the bill when he paid for the repair."

"Can we see it?" Tom asked.

"All right, if you want to," the man said. "It's on the table in the back room. Be careful, it's kind of dark back there."

They found a small, windowless room all the way in the back.

"That looks like the bill on the table," Alice said, walking over to it. Just as she did, a heavy door slammed shut behind them.

They ran back to the door and tried to get it open, but they couldn't find a knob or latch on the inside. They were locked in!

Turn to page 14.

Blackstone waited a few minutes until he was sure that the men were gone, then he quickly undid the ropes that tied his hands.

"Wow!" Tom exclaimed. "How did you do that?"

"Magicians," Blackstone said, "are not the easiest people to keep tied up. One of our basic skills is being able to free ourselves. Houdini, the famous magician, was the greatest escape artist that ever lived."

Blackstone went to the door and listened for a few moments. Then he untied Tom and Alice, and took a small penknife out of his pocket. He opened up the knife, one blade of which was long and very thin. He slipped the blade into the keyhole of the door. There was a faint click, and Blackstone opened the door a crack and carefully looked through.

"The coast is clear," he said, opening the door all the way.

Turn to page 38.

The inside of the room was now pitch dark. They pounded on the inside of the door, but there was no answer. They waited there in the darkness, banging on the door every few minutes. Gradually, their eyes got used to the very faint light coming from a small hole high up on the wall.

"Let's try to find some way to get out of here," Tom said.

"There could be some place on the floor—or the ceiling," Alice added. "It's worth a try, anyway."

They searched all around. Finally, they found a small groove on the floor that looked like part of a trapdoor. It was, but they had to move a whole pile of boxes out of the way to uncover it. The trapdoor opened up with a loud, squeaking sound—as if it hadn't been opened in years. There was a ladder going down.

"It sure is dark down there," Alice said.

"It could be a way out, though," Tom said.

"I think we can wait here for just a while longer," Alice said with a shudder. "It looks too spooky for me."

"Right," said Tom. "We won't go down there unless we have to."

"Let's try the door again," Alice said. "There *must* be a way to get it open."

They started toward the door. Suddenly it started to slowly open. Tom and Alice were frozen to the spot. There was a figure in the dim light just outside the door. At first they couldn't see who it was. Then they did. It was Blackstone the magician.

"Mr. Blackstone, it's Tom and Alice Kingsley!" Alice exclaimed. "Are we glad to see you!"

"I'm just as glad to see you," Blackstone said. "I was asking for you and your father at the hotel. They told me that you had gone to look for him. When I got to the garage I found this on the ground out in front."

"Why, that's my scarf!" Alice exclaimed. "I didn't even realize that I had dropped it."

"I'm glad you did," Tom said.

"How did you know it was mine?" Alice asked.

"I didn't," Blackstone said. "It was just a hunch. There was no one around, so I decided to do some snooping."

"We found a trapdoor on the other side of this room," said Alice. "We were trying to decide if we should go down there. Then you came and—"

"A trapdoor!" Blackstone interrupted. "I have another hunch. It might be interesting to see what's down there."

"I know," Alice said, "but somehow I'd rather start searching for Dad."

If they explore the tunnel, turn to page 17.

If they leave the garage and start their search for Mr. Kingsley, turn to page 42.

"If we investigate what's down there," Blackstone said, "it could give us a clue as to what is going on here. I think your father's disappearance and your being locked in this room are somehow connected."

"All right," said Alice. "As long as you go first."

Blackstone took a small but powerful flashlight out of his pocket and shined it down into the darkness beneath the trapdoor. Then he went down the ladder with Tom and Alice following.

"This is a tunnel!" Blackstone exclaimed. "I thought it might be. It goes straight in the direction of Stonehenge."

"Do you think it could go all the way there?" Tom asked.

"I doubt it," Blackstone said. "Stonehenge is a good two miles away. But we'll follow it anyway and see where it *does* go."

They walked single file in the narrow, low ceilinged tunnel for what seemed like a long time. Blackstone led the way, the beam of his flashlight stabbing into the darkness ahead. Then he suddenly stopped, putting his finger to his lips to indicate silence.

"I hear voices from somewhere," he whispered. "They seem to be coming from somewhere in front of and above us."

Blackstone shined the beam of his flashlight upward on the roof of the tunnel as he made his way slowly forward. Then he stopped and snapped off his flashlight.

"We're right below another trapdoor," he whispered even more softly.

The voices were much louder now.

"We have to keep them out of the way until after the ceremony," one of the voices said.

"Right. If they come snooping around at the wrong time, they could mess up the whole thing," said another.

"But I'm worried about holding those kids," said the first voice. "We could be charged with kidnapping and—"

"Don't worry!" the other voice interrupted. "If they locked themselves in the back room of the garage, that's their fault. We'll let them out tomorrow."

"Doesn't that room have an old, unused entrance to the Druid tunnel?" asked the first voice.

"Yes, but no one will ever find it, I'm sure. It's hidden under a stack of boxes."

"Well, you'd better be sure . . ." the voice trailed off.

Tom, Alice, and Blackstone could hear the footsteps on the floor above leaving.

"Do you think we should climb up through this trapdoor?" Tom asked. "Or should we keep going down this tunnel?"

If they decide to climb up, turn to page 25.

If they keep going in the tunnel,
turn to page 20.

"It might be better if we keep going down this tunnel," Blackstone said. "They called it the 'Druid tunnel.' I'd like to know why."

Blackstone clicked his flashlight on again, and they all started down the tunnel. After a while, the walls of the tunnel were no longer made of rough, jagged stone but changed to large, smooth rectangular blocks carefully fitted together. Far up ahead they saw a small but bright circle of light.

After another few minutes of walking, they came out into a circular clearing surrounded by oak trees.

"This is the kind of clearing where the ancient Druids held their religious services," Blackstone said. "Of course that was thousands of years ago. But I wonder if—"

Blackstone's thought was cut short by a crashing sound in the woods nearby. The sounds were getting louder—in fact, heading in their direction.

Three men entered the clearing. One of them was Mr. Kingsley! The other two were dressed in long white robes with hoods that covered their heads and faces.

"Dad!" Alice cried, running out to her father.

Tom and Blackstone followed her. The two men in the robes pushed back their hoods and had wide grins on their faces.

"My friends here," said Mr. Kingsley, pointing to the men in the robes, "are modern day Druids. That is, they're not *real* Druids, but they like to keep the memory of the old ways alive. Every year, they help put on a big pageant at Stonehenge."

"We were worried when you didn't come back to the hotel," Alice said. "We came looking for you."

"I figured you might," said Mr. Kingsley. "That's why I gave the man at the garage a note to send back to you, but I guess you never received it."

"The garage man!" exclaimed one of the robed men. "That would be old Grimsey. He and some of his friends have been in the Druid pageant too long. Now they think they really *are* Druids. They must think that you are here to try to stop the ceremony. But never mind, we can take care of them. All of you are invited to Stonehenge tonight. I'll provide the robes for you all. I know you'll like the pageant."

THE END

Blackstone headed the plane back toward the small airport. The fighter plane followed close behind, but it turned in the other direction as soon as they headed down toward the landing strip.

When they landed, Blackstone went to ask the airport manager if he knew anything about the World War II fighter plane that had been after them.

"That's crazy McInter," said the manager. "He's harmless enough, even though we can't seem to stop him from buzzing other planes now and then. I should have warned you about him."

Blackstone, Tom, and Alice drove back to the hotel where they found Mr. Kingsley waiting for them. He was upset that they didn't get the note he had sent telling them that he would be delayed.

However, everything worked out all right. That night,

after a good dinner in the hotel restaurant, they all drove over to Stonehenge where many of the local people dressed up in costumes and reenacted the ancient Druid ceremonies.

THE END

Tom, Alice, and Blackstone waited for a few minutes until they were sure that it was absolutely quiet above.

"Here, put your foot in my cupped hand," Blackstone said to Alice, "and I'll boost you up so that you can push the trapdoor open."

It worked like a charm. Blackstone lifted first Alice and then Tom through the opening. After that, Blackstone reached up and grabbed the edge of the trapdoor with his fingertips and, with one quick motion, flipped himself up through the opening.

"That's great!" Tom exclaimed. "How did you do that?"

"Just a little trick I learned a while back," Blackstone said. "Magicians must master many arts including that of acrobatics."

They were in a large, almost empty barn. Over on one side was a long coat rack with a collection of white robes with hoods. Piled in front of these were a number of wooden staffs, each made from a long, twisted length of branch, stripped of its bark and polished. And next to these was another pile—this one of unlit torches.

"Looks like we have the makings of a Druid parade," Blackstone said.

Suddenly a deep voice came from the door of the barn: "So we've caught some trespassers snooping around."

Several men were standing there—and each had a weapon in his hand.

"One of them is the man from the garage," Tom whispered to Blackstone.

"I suspected as much," Blackstone whispered back.

"Be quiet!" ordered one of the men. "Turn around and put your hands together behind your back. We're going to tie you up."

The men, under the direction of the man from the garage, quickly tied up Tom, Alice, and Blackstone. After they had tied their hands, they herded them into a small side room and made them sit down on the floor where they tied their feet together. They did it like they really knew what they were doing.

As the men went away, they closed and locked the door.

Turn to page 13.

Tom and Alice waited at the hotel. After a while, they *really* started to get worried.

"Maybe we should try to get hold of Mr. Blackstone," Alice said.

"If we knew where he was," Tom said. "All we know is that he's giving a performance for the royal family."

"Do you think we could call Buckingham Palace?" Alice asked. "I *think* that's where the royal family lives."

"You can't just call Buckingham Palace," said Tom. "That's like trying to call the White House back home."

"I'm going to try anyway," Alice said. "We've got nothing to lose by trying."

Alice went to the hotel phone in the lobby and dialed the operator. "Yes, operator," she said in a loud voice. "I want to call Blackstone the magician. He should be at Buckingham Palace."

"He may be a lot closer than that," a voice came from behind her.

"Mr. Blackstone, how did you get here?" Alice asked excitedly.

"Don't you know that magicians appear like magic?" Blackstone said.

"We're *so* glad to see you," Alice said. "Dad's been gone for hours and we're getting a little scared."

"I have a car parked outside," Blackstone said. "Let's see if we can find your father."

Tom and Alice jumped into the back of the car, and Blackstone roared away from the front of the hotel. Almost immediately they were out of town and into the countryside.

After a few minutes of driving, Blackstone said,

"Here's a garage coming up. Let's see if anyone there has any information about your father."

As Blackstone's car pulled to a stop in front of the garage, they saw a man seated in a chair next to a large door.

"Did a small car stop here a few hours ago for repairs?" Blackstone asked.

"Might have," said the man, getting up from his chair and stretching. "I wouldn't know, though, I just got here. None of the other mechanics will be here until tomorrow."

"Thanks anyway," Tom said as they all got back into the car and started off again. And thanks for nothing, Tom thought to himself.

"That man was lying about just getting there," Blackstone said. "The way he got up from that chair and

"I don't blame you at all," said Blackstone. "We'll make another pass over Stonehenge so that we can take another look."

Suddenly, another small plane roared by—very close. Small flashes of light were coming from the front of it.

"What the—" Blackstone exclaimed. "That's a World War II fighter plane—and it was firing at us!"

The fighter plane was in the distance, making a tight turn in the air so that it could make another pass.

"Oh my!" Alice exclaimed. "Are they going to shoot us down?"

"No, I don't think so," said Blackstone. "They could have easily done that the first time they went by. I think they are just trying to scare us."

"They're doing a good job of that," said Tom. "What'll we do?"

"There are several things we can do," Blackstone said. "We can make an emergency landing, go back to the small airport, or see if this plane can fly faster than that one."

If they make an emergency landing,
turn to page 35.

If they go back to the airport, turn to page 23.

If they try to outfly the other plane,
turn to page 61.

Blackstone dove the plane down toward the ground. Just as it looked as if they were going to crash, he brought the nose of the plane up and they were skimming along just above the ground.

"That stretch of pasture up ahead looks about as smooth as any we can find around here," Blackstone said.

The wheels of the plane touched the ground and the plane bumped along for a short while and then came to a stop.

"We were lucky we didn't hit a rock—or a cow," Blackstone said as they all got out of the plane.

Just as they did, the fighter plane came roaring by again just over their heads—and then vanished into the distance.

"Why did it *do* that?" Alice asked.

"Maybe there is something someone doesn't want us to see from the air," Blackstone said. "Like preparations nearby for a ceremony they would rather keep secret."

"Is that Stonehenge over there?" Alice asked, pointing to a formation of large stones rising up into the air about a mile away.

"That's it," Blackstone said.

"You mean all this fuss is over that pile of *stones!*"

"Today they are just a ruin," said Blackstone, "but when they were put up thousands of years ago, they were the religious center of a vast area."

"That may be true, but . . . but . . ." said Alice, pulling at Blackstone's sleeve and pointing. "I think we're in trouble!"

Turn to page 55.

Blackstone's plane bounced to a stop not far from the wreck of the fighter plane. A column of smoke was rising from it, and the pilot was next to it, a fire extinguisher in his hands. His long gray hair spilled down below his World War II flight helmet. Blackstone jumped out of his plane and ran over to him. Tom and Alice followed.

"Are you all right?" Blackstone asked.

"Sure am, except for my plane which looks like a total loss," the pilot said. "You shot me down fair and square. There's not many that can force down the great Ian McInter."

"We didn't—" Tom started.

"It's all right," Blackstone interrupted. "I'm sorry about your plane," he said to McInter.

"Shot me down fair and square," McInter mumbled, turning away to hide the tears in his eyes.

Blackstone led Tom and Alice back to his plane.

"Serves him right for scaring us that way," Alice said.

"I think he's living in the past," Blackstone said sadly. "And speaking of the past, let's get over to Stonehenge and see if we can solve another mystery."

THE END

Blackstone walked toward the door of the large barn. He stopped at the side of the door and looked cautiously outside. He was just in time to see a large car vanishing down the long driveway in the direction of the main road.

"I think it's safe to go out," he said. "The garage is probably close by."

"We're going back to the garage!" Alice exclaimed.

"We'll be all right as long as we're careful," Blackstone said.

After a few minutes of walking they found the garage. Fortunately, Blackstone's car was still there. They all got in and drove toward Salisbury.

They were almost to Salisbury when a small red car passed them going the other way.

"Hey! Stop!" Alice yelled. "That was Dad driving that car!"

Blackstone made a tight turn on the highway and headed in the other direction after Mr. Kingsley's car.

"Can you catch up with Dad?" Tom asked.

"No problem," said Blackstone. "This car is twice as fast as the one your father is driving."

Just as he said that, a car even larger than Blackstone's roared up from behind them and pretended to try to pass. Instead of passing, the new car deliberately swerved sideways, smashing into the side of Blackstone's car—trying to drive it off the road. Even though Blackstone was caught by surprise, he was too good a driver to be pushed off the road that easily. He slammed on the brakes and at the same time bumped his front fender violently against the back of the other car. The other car weaved back and forth a couple of times, then veered off the road and turned over.

Blackstone brought his car to a stop, then he jumped out and ran over to the other car. The two men in the car were badly shaken up but were otherwise unhurt. Just as they crawled out, a third car pulled up to the side of the road and a uniformed constable got out and came over.

"I saw the whole thing from up the road," he said. "If I'm not mistaken, these are two of the local characters who fancy themselves to be real Druids. I've had my eye on them for some time. They're always causing some sort of trouble, but this time they've gone too far. I'm taking them straight to jail."

Tom, Alice, and Blackstone got back into their car—a bit dented now on one side, but still running—and drove back to town. Mr. Kingsley was there waiting for them at the hotel.

"We found a couple of Druids, Dad," Alice said.

"Or rather, they found us," said Blackstone, laughing.

"Well, I have news for all of you," said Mr. Kingsley. "There's going to be a big Druid ceremony tonight at Stonehenge—and we're all going."

THE END

Tom, Alice, and Blackstone left the garage. There was still no one there.

"I wonder who's minding the store," Blackstone said. "There's something fishy going on here. I think I'll take another look around."

And it was a good thing that he did. Way off under a bush, he found a small, crumpled up piece of paper. He opened it up and smoothed it out. It said:

Dear Tom and Alice,

I'll be very late in getting back to the hotel. Enjoy yourselves in town and have a good dinner in the hotel restaurant. If Blackstone shows up, tell him to meet me at Stonehenge at midnight.

Love,
Dad

Blackstone showed the note to Tom and Alice.

"Stonehenge at midnight!" Tom exclaimed. "Can we go too? Can—"

"Slow down!" Blackstone interrupted. "I have to think about this. To start with, I don't think you locked yourselves in that room accidentally. You were tricked into going in there. And where is the garage man? Your father seems to have entrusted him with a note which was not delivered, in fact, thrown away. Midnight is still a long way off. I know a friendly pub in town where we can wait. Maybe I can show you a few magic tricks."

"Oh will you!" Alice said. "That sounds great."

"Can Alice and I really go into a pub?" Tom asked. "Aren't they like bars back home?"

"Nothing like that," Blackstone said. "The pubs here are for the whole family. But you'll see."

They all got into Blackstone's car and in a matter of minutes were back in town.

The pub was full of people, and Tom and Alice were happy to see children of all ages. Off in one corner, several men were tossing darts at a circular target hung on the wall. Blackstone found a table for them in another corner.

"First," Blackstone said, "we'll eat some fish and chips."

"Oh my!" Alice said in alarm.

"Don't worry," Blackstone said. "Chips are what we call French fries back home."

After they had finished eating, Blackstone took a coin—a dime—out of his pocket. "Watch this," he said, and with that, he raised his arm and tossed the coin down his sleeve. Then with the other hand, he pulled the dime back out at the elbow.

"That's easy," Alice said. "You've just got a hole in your sleeve at the elbow."

"Take a look," Blackstone said, holding out his arm.

Tom and Alice both examined the sleeve very carefully.

"You're right," Tom said. "There's nothing wrong with your sleeve at all. How did you do that?"

"Just a little misdirection," Blackstone said. "You see, before I threw the coin down my sleeve, I stuck a different dime against the button of my cuff. When I reached down to draw the coin out of my sleeve, I was actually drawing *that* one down the back of my arm. It only *looked* like it came out at my elbow."

The rest of the afternoon and evening were spent talking with and being entertained by Blackstone. Time went by so quickly that they were surprised when Blackstone looked at his watch and said, "I think it's getting close to midnight. The two of you can go with me to Stonehenge, but we'd better be very careful. You're not tired, are you?"

"No! No!" Tom exclaimed. "I'm wide awake."

"Me too," Alice said.

"In that case," Blackstone said, "we'd better get moving."

They all went outside and jumped into Blackstone's car. As they headed out of town, a full moon hung overhead, bathing everything in a silvery light. As they passed the garage, it looked dark and spooky with coal black shadows behind it.

"I'm sure glad we aren't locked up in there anymore," Alice said.

A few minutes after passing the garage, Blackstone slowed down the car.

"I want to park away from Stonehenge and approach it carefully," he said. "We don't really know what's going on there."

Blackstone pulled off the main highway and went a short way down a small dirt road. There was another car parked there.

"Hey!" said Alice. "That looks like the car that Dad was driving."

"I thought as much," Blackstone said. "He must be somewhere close by."

They started running across the field which was almost as bright as day in the moonlight.

As they got closer to Stonehenge, they could see its

stone columns rising jet black against the silvery fields beyond it in the moonlight. Then, suddenly, a ring of burning torches flared up around the distant stones. They could hear a strange chanting being carried across the fields on the wind.

"There's definitely some kind of ceremony going on there," Blackstone said. "It might not be safe to get any closer."

"We're still really far away," Tom said. "I don't think it would hurt for us to get a little closer."

If they stay where they are, turn to page 48.

If they go closer to the ceremony, turn to page 51.

They stood there for a few minutes staring toward Stonehenge. Then they heard footsteps nearby. A dark silhouette loomed in the moonlight. Tom and Alice were frightened for a moment and then they both recognized who it was.

"Dad!" they both yelled. "We're over here."

"Am I ever glad to see you two," said Mr. Kingsley. "And you too, Blackstone. I knew you'd have no trouble finding me."

"I hope you don't mind that I brought the kids," Blackstone said.

"Not at all," Mr. Kingsley said. "I think it's safe enough as long as we keep our distance. And you all may be in for a surprise in a few minutes."

"What surprise, Dad?" Alice asked.

"This afternoon," Mr. Kingsley said, "when I was driving to the garage, a thought suddenly came to me. So I left a note with the garage man—he promised to leave it for you at the hotel—and drove over to Salisbury to check my hunch in the library there. And I was right—look at the moon!"

Tom and Alice looked up and saw the moon was slowly starting to disappear.

"Aha! It's an eclipse!" Blackstone said. "I should have known. You know there are those who claim that Stonehenge is a kind of computer that the ancients used to tell when an eclipse was going to happen."

A high-pitched drone went up in the distance and the torches went out.

"The Druids are having their ceremony," Mr. Kingsley said.

"That's all very well," said Blackstone, "but the

Druids didn't build Stonehenge. They took it over long after the very ancient people who built it had vanished."

"There are also those who say that the wizard Merlin brought its stones from Ireland by magic," said Mr. Kingsley.

"Really?" Alice said.

"I'd take that one with a grain of salt," said Blackstone, laughing.

As they were talking, the moon grew smaller and smaller until it was only a thin crescent. Then it began to grow again.

As soon as the moon was fully back, the highway from Stonehenge became filled with a long line of headlights heading back toward town.

"Do you think the Druids drive cars?" Tom asked.

"Maybe they do," said Blackstone. "Or maybe it's a lot of people who would like to be Druids. Anyway, I don't think you'll ever forget tonight."

And he was right.

THE END

They all went carefully forward. Suddenly, they were surrounded by men in white robes—and all carrying pitchforks. The men looked angry and were mumbling in a strange language. Tom and Alice did catch the word "sacrifice" a couple of times.

"Oh my!" Alice said. "Do you think they would really sacrifice us?"

"They'd probably like to," said Blackstone, "but I don't think they'd risk it in this day and age."

The Druids prodded them across the field and right up to and among the tall stones of Stonehenge—then up to a large horizontal stone.

"This looks like a sacrificial altar!" Tom said, his voice shaking.

"Don't worry," Blackstone whispered. "If it's a show they want, I'll give them one."

Blackstone stepped forward and lifted his hand. Suddenly, there was a bright, blinding flash and a big cloud of white smoke formed around him. When the smoke cleared, Blackstone had vanished, but you could hear his laughter. It sounded like it was coming from within the stones themselves.

All of the Druids dropped their pitchforks and took off in terror across the fields. Soon, Tom and Alice were alone. Blackstone slipped out from a narrow space between two of the stones.

"I guess the combination of my trick and the eclipse was too much for them," Blackstone said.

"The eclipse?" Alice said.

"Yes," Blackstone said. "Look at the moon. It's starting to vanish. Now that's what I call good timing."

"Hello!" a familiar voice called out from outside the stones. It was Mr. Kingsley. "What happened?" he

asked. "I was nearly trampled by stampeding Druids."

"Just a little anti-Druid magic," Blackstone said. "I do the same trick on the stage all the time."

"You'll have to teach us how to do that one," Tom said.

"Maybe I will," Blackstone said, "someday."

THE END

Not far away across the field a large bull was eyeing the three of them and beginning to paw the ground with one of his front feet.

"Oh my!" Tom said. "What'll we do?"

"If we keep calm," said Blackstone, "everything will be all right. The highway is not far away over to our right. On the other hand, it might be interesting to find out if this bull has ever seen any magic tricks."

"Don't worry," Blackstone said. "I've always wanted to try this. Just stay behind me."

Blackstone stepped forward toward the bull. The bull eyed him up and down, snorting a few times, and then charged. Blackstone raised his arm and a long red scarf shot out to one side of him and hung in the air. Then another scarf shot out from the other side. Then another—and another. All the scarves seemed to hang in the air. The bull stopped its charge and stood there, its head moving from side to side trying to figure out what was going on. Then the scarves began to vanish and reappear in different places. The bull sat down on the ground and refused to look.

Blackstone motioned with his hand and Tom and Alice followed him past the bull and over to a fence on the far side of the field, which they climbed over to safety—or at least they thought it was safe.

No sooner were they over the fence, than they were surrounded by a dozen men with angry expressions on their faces.

"You are trespassing on our land," said one of them, "and we should make an example of you. You come here, carve your initials on our sacred stones, and throw rubbish all over our fields."

"On the contrary," Blackstone said, "we have noth-

ing but respect for your monuments. Anyone who does anything to damage them is very wrong."

"Glad to hear you say that," said another of the men. "Perhaps we have misjudged you. In fact, if you'd like to come to our ceremony tonight at Stonehenge, you're welcome. We dress up like Druids and act out the ancient ways among the stones."

Blackstone thanked the men and he, Tom, and Alice waved good-bye as the men went back to their fields. The Stonehenge Information Center was not far away. There Blackstone, Tom, and Alice took a bus back to town. Mr. Kingsley was at the hotel waiting for them. He had just gotten back from Stonehenge himself. Somehow they had all just missed each other and they had not gotten his note.

That night they all went back out to Stonehenge to see the ceremony. It was an experience they'd never forget.

THE END

"I think I'd like to stay on the ground," Alice said.

"All right, then," Blackstone said, "let's drive over to Stonehenge and look around. Maybe we'll find your father on the way."

"That sounds great," Tom said.

After a short drive, they saw what looked like a pile of large stones just off the side of the road up ahead.

"That's Stonehenge," Blackstone said.

"*That's* Stonehenge?" Alice asked.

"It doesn't look like much from here," Blackstone said. "But it will be much more interesting when we get up close. First we'll have to park."

They pulled into a parking lot on the side of the road.

"That car over there!" Alice said. "It looks like the car that Dad rented."

"It looks like it, all right," Tom said. "Do you think he came here without us?"

"Well, we'll find out soon," Blackstone said. "But first we'll have to wait in that line up ahead. They only let a few people go near the ruins at a time."

Not only was there a line, it was a *long* line.

"How about some candy while we're waiting," Blackstone said, taking out an empty drinking glass from his pocket.

"That's just an empty glass," Alice said.

"It won't be for long," Blackstone said, taking out a handkerchief and draping it over the glass.

Blackstone pulled away the handkerchief and suddenly the glass was filled with candy.

"Hey! That's a neat trick," Tom said. "I wish *I* could do that."

"It's a very simple trick," Blackstone said. "When

you've finished eating the candy, I'll show you how it's done. But don't eat too fast."

When they finished the candy, they were almost at the entrance to the ruins.

"Now will you show us how to do it?" Alice asked, visions of a bottomless jar of candy dancing in her head.

"I'm afraid it's not what you think," Blackstone said, seeing the gleam in her eyes.

He took out a small piece of plastic, mirrored on one side, and slipped it into the glass—dividing the inside of the glass neatly in half.

"Now lend me your ring," Blackstone said.

Alice slipped the ring off of her finger and handed it to Blackstone, who dropped it into one side of the glass. The ring seemed to vanish.

"You see, the mirror makes you think that you are looking at an empty glass," Blackstone said.

He put the handkerchief back over the glass and pulled it away, pulling out the plastic divider with it. The ring magically reappeared. Blackstone handed it back to Alice. She had a disappointed look on her face.

"I told you it was a trick," Blackstone said. "Now it's our turn to go over to the ruins."

The Stonehenge ruins were on the other side of the highway. They all went through a tunnel under the road and walked toward the stones which now towered over them. And there was Mr. Kingsley off to one side—staring at the stones with total concentration.

Alice went over and tugged at his sleeve. Mr. Kingsley looked back with a startled look on his face. "Tom! Alice! And Blackstone!" he said. "I lost all track of time out here. I was going to come back to the hotel and get you for the big pageant they're going to have here tonight."

"I don't care about that," Alice said. "I'm just glad that we found you."

"Found me?" said Mr. Kingsley. "Didn't you get my note?"

"I'm afraid they didn't," said Blackstone. "They were very worried and—"

"I'm really sorry," Mr. Kingsley interrupted. "I hope the performance of the Druids tonight will make up for everything."

And it did!

THE END

"This plane has a lot of power," Blackstone said. "Let's see if that antique can keep up with us."

Blackstone put his plane into a dive to pick up speed, then zoomed away over the fields below. The fighter plane was right behind, staying on their tail.

"That plane is faster than I thought," Blackstone said. "But we'll see how long it can keep up with us."

Blackstone pulled up and dived again. Tom and Alice felt like they were on a roller coaster. The other plane was still right behind them, but suddenly it began to leave a trail of black smoke and dropped back as it lost air speed.

"I think that plane is in trouble," Blackstone said, banking hard to the right to get a better look.

The other plane dropped lower and lower. Finally it crash landed on the ground down below them.

If Blackstone makes an emergency landing to see if the pilot of the other plane is all right, turn to page 37.

If he flies to the main airport at Salisbury to have the authorities send help, turn to page 9.

THE DISAPPEARING COIN
YOUR OWN MAGIC TRICK

Step 1: Out of sight of your audience, slip a small, thin rubber band over your thumb and forefinger. Facing the audience, quickly pass a handkerchief over this hand and press out a small pocket into the center of the rubber band.

Step 2: Borrow a coin from someone in the audience, and place it in the center of the handkerchief—in reality, putting it on top of the pocket you have made with your fingers and the rubber band.

Step 3: Flip the handkerchief into the air, at the same time being careful to let the rubber band snap closed around the top of the pocket you made, trapping the coin inside.

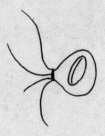

Step 4: It looks as though the coin has vanished. Shake out the handkerchief to show the coin is gone.

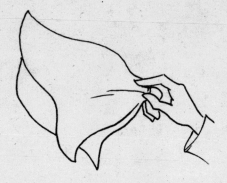

Step 5: When you put the handkerchief away, carefully slip the coin out and produce it elsewhere.